MAGICALLY MAXIMUS

MAGICALLY
MAXIMUS

By Kiki Thorpe

Illustrated by Laura Catrinella

DISNEP · HYPERION
Los Angeles   New York

First Edition, June 2022
10 9 8 7 6 5 4 3 2 1
FAC-020093-22119
Printed in the United States of America

This book is set in Goudy Old Style Std/Monotype; Laughing Gull/Atlantic Fonts
Designed by Samantha Krause

Library of Congress Cataloging-in-Publication Data

Names: Thorpe, Kiki, author.
Title: Magically Maximus / by Kiki Thorpe. Illustrated by Laura Catrinella.
Description: First edition. • Los Angeles : Disney-Hyperion, 2022. •
 Series: Horsetail hollow ; book 1 • Audience: Ages 5–8. • Audience:
 Grades 2–3. • Summary: Eight-year-old Maddie and her family move to a
 farm called Horsetail Hollow, and after she and her six-year-old sister, Evie,
 find a wishing well, a magnificent white horse appears—but Maximus is a
 fairy-tale horse, conjured out of Evie's book—so when the girls try to
 wish him back into his story, they all end up in the fairy tale, trying
 to save Rapunzel.
Identifiers: LCCN 2021041735 • ISBN 9781368072137 (hardcover) • ISBN
 9781368072274 (trade paperback) • ISBN 9781368073936 (ebook)
Subjects: LCSH: Tangled (Motion picture)—Juvenile fiction. •
 Magic—Juvenile fiction. • Sisters—Juvenile fiction. • Wishes—Juvenile
 fiction. • Horses—Juvenile fiction. • Fairy tales—Adaptation. • CYAC:
 Characters in literature—Fiction. • Magic—Fiction. • Sisters—Fiction.
 • Wishes—Fiction. • Horses—Fiction. • Fairy tales—Adaptations. •
 Horses—Fiction. • Fairy tales. • LCGFT: Fairy tales.
Classification: LCC PZ7.T3974 Maj 2022 • DDC [Fic]—dc23
LC record available at https://lccn.loc.gov/2021041735

Reinforced binding
Visit www.DisneyBooks.com

For Dijon and Stretch

Maddie Phillips sat cross-legged on her bed. Pennies, nickels, dimes, quarters, and a few crumpled bills were spread across the quilt. An empty jar lay on its side next to her.

Maddie leaned forward, counting. "Seventy-six, seventy-seven, seventy-eight, seventy-nine . . . thirty-six dollars and seventy-nine cents."

Maddie put her chin in her hand. She blew a curl off her forehead with an unhappy sigh. Thirty-six

dollars and seventy-nine cents was not even enough to buy a saddle. Much less a horse.

Maddie looked out the window. From her bedroom she could see an old barn and a fenced paddock. She could see fields overgrown with weeds and a little pond ringed with reedy horsetail plants.

"Horsetail Hollow," Maddie muttered. "Some name for a farm with no horse."

When her parents had told her they were moving to an old farmhouse in the country, Maddie thought her dreams had finally come true. She had imagined chickens and goats and a big vegetable garden. But most of all, she'd imagined a horse.

It would be a beautiful chestnut, maybe, or a shining blond palomino. She would name it Lucky or Wild Rose, and it would come running when she called. She would pet its soft nose and feed it carrots and apples. Maddie could see it so clearly in her mind.

But nothing had turned out the way she'd imagined. The farmhouse was very old. The roof leaked. The porch sagged. There were mice in the attic and weeds in the garden. Every day, Maddie's parents worked hard to fix it. They patched and painted. They hammered and sanded. They weeded and mowed. They seemed even busier now than they had been when they lived in the city.

And there was no time—or money—for a horse. The only animal was a grumpy goat named Ramsey that had come with the place.

But Horsetail Hollow had everything a horse could want. It had a barn and a pasture—and now it had Maddie! She had read every horse book. She'd watched every horse movie. She'd spent three summers at Sunny Stables Horse-Riding Day Camp. At nine, she was practically a horse expert! She knew she was destined to have her own horse.

She just had to figure out how.

Maddie jumped as the door to her room burst open. Her six-year-old sister, Evie, walked in, wobbling in a pair of high-heeled shoes. She was

dressed in a blue satin gown and elbow-length gloves. A plastic jeweled crown sparkled atop her dark brown curls.

"Let's play Princess!" Evie exclaimed. She spied the coins and bills on Maddie's bed. Her blue eyes widened. "Ooh! Treasure!"

"It's not treasure. It's *savings*." Maddie scooped up the money. She stuffed it back in the jar and screwed the lid on tight.

"You missed one." Evie picked up a penny off the floor. She handed it to Maddie.

Maddie put the penny in her pocket. "Evie, you know the rule. You're supposed to knock," she grumbled.

Evie knocked on the open door. "Come on. *Please*, Maddie? I'll let you wear my crown."

"No thanks," Maddie said.

"I know! I can braid your hair." Evie went to her and started to loosen the band on Maddie's long, dark ponytail.

"Evie, stop!" Maddie pushed her hand away. Evie liked to try fancy hairstyles that turned Maddie's hair into a tangled mess. Maddie preferred her ponytail. It was simple, but at least it was neat.

Evie folded her arms. "Will you read to me, then?"

Maddie sighed. "Not now. I'm busy."

Evie looked around the tidy bedroom. "Doing what?"

"I'm going to the barn." Maddie liked the old barn. The hayloft was a good place to daydream.

"Can I come?" Evie asked.

Maddie thought about it. Mom was working in the home office. Maddie could hear the keyboard going *clickity-click*. Dad was hammering somewhere in the house.

If she said no, Evie might make a fuss. Then the clicking and hammering would stop. And their parents would probably give them chores.

"Okay," Maddie agreed. "But you have to wear real shoes."

"Be right back!" Evie raced from the room.

She returned a minute later, wearing sneakers. A thick, heavy book with a worn cover was tucked under her arm.

"What's that?" Maddie asked.

Evie gave her a dimpled smile. "Fairy tales. Just in case you change your mind about reading."

"Don't count on it," said Maddie.

They made their way out the back door and

across the yard. On the way to the barn, they passed Ramsey's pen.

"MAAAH!" the old goat bleated. He lowered his horns and rammed the gate.

Both girls jumped. Ramsey looked pleased. His greatest joy was hitting things with his head.

"I hate it when he does that," Evie said.

"Just be glad he's on the other side of the fence," said Maddie.

When they got to the barn, Maddie pulled open the big wooden door. Inside, it was dark and quiet. Beams of sunlight peeked between the boards. The wooden floor creaked under their feet.

A burst of flapping overhead made Maddie jump. But it was just a pair of barn swallows, disturbed from their nest.

One side of the barn held some rusty farm equipment. The other side had a row of stalls. Maddie knew they'd once held horses. She'd found grooming brushes among some old tools that had been left behind.

Maddie walked over to the stalls and peeked inside. Maybe she would find a horseshoe to hang on her wall for good luck. But the stalls were empty except for some dusty-looking straw on the floor.

"What's up here?" Evie said behind her.

Maddie turned. She saw the hem of Evie's skirt disappearing up the ladder to the hayloft.

"Careful, Evie!" Maddie went to the ladder and climbed up after her.

The loft held a few rows of stacked hay bales. More loose hay was piled on the floor.

Evie climbed onto a stack of hay bales and jumped. She landed on her bottom in a pile of hay.

"Try it, Maddie!" Evie said. "It's like jumping into clouds."

It did look sort of fun. Maddie climbed onto a stack of hay bales and jumped. She plopped into a pile of hay, landing next to Evie.

Evie held up the book of fairy tales. "Now will you read to me?"

Maddie sighed. "Okay, *one* story."

Evie chewed her lip, thinking. "Rapunzel," she said at last.

Maddie turned to "The Story of Rapunzel." "'Once upon a time, in a faraway kingdom, a princess was born with magical golden hair. And she was called Rapunzel. . . .'"

As Maddie read the part about the witch kidnapping the baby Rapunzel, Evie scowled. When she read how the whole kingdom searched for the princess, to no avail, Evie's brow furrowed with worry. No matter how many times she'd heard it, Evie never tired of the story. She hung on every word as if Rapunzel were her own dear friend.

Maddie, on the other hand, couldn't read fast enough. She rushed through the words, quickly flipping the pages. Fairy tales bored her.

"'And she might have stayed lost forever, were it

not for a thief, who happened upon the tower in the woods,'" Maddie read.

She paused. In the picture, four palace guards on horseback chased the thief through the woods. Maddie gazed longingly at the white horse with a cream-colored mane. She would love to have a horse like that.

Evie poked her. "Keep reading."

"And the prince found Rapunzel, and he rescued her from the tower, and they all lived happily ever after. The end." Maddie snapped the book shut.

"Maddie!" Evie wailed. "That's not how it goes!"

"Read the rest yourself," Maddie said. "You already know it by heart."

Leaving Evie in the hay, Maddie got up and walked over to the open hayloft door. The door was like a big square window cut out of the side of the barn. From here, she could see the whole farm and the surrounding woods.

Not far from the barn, Maddie spied something

she'd never noticed before: a little roof peeking up above the high, overgrown grass.

"What's that?" she wondered aloud.

"What's what?" Evie asked, coming over to see.

"There, by those trees." Maddie pointed.

"It looks like an itty-bitty house," Evie said.

"I'm going to see what it is." Maddie headed for the ladder, and Evie scrambled after her.

When they got there, Maddie saw the roof didn't belong to a house. It sat above an old well. The well looked like something out of Evie's fairy-tale book. It had a round stone wall and a wooden bucket. The shingles on the roof were covered in moss.

"A wishing well!" Evie cried, running to it.

Maddie rolled her eyes. "It's a *real* well, Evie. Farms have those kinds of things."

A few rotted wooden boards covered the opening. Maddie moved them aside. She peered down into the darkness, but she couldn't see the bottom. The well was very deep.

Evie set the book of fairy tales on the low stone wall. She leaned her elbows on the side and looked down, too.

"Careful, Evie. Don't lean so far." Maddie pulled her back from the edge.

"I wish I had a penny so I could make a wish," Evie said.

Maddie remembered the penny in her pocket. She was about to hand it to Evie. Then she hesitated.

Why should Evie have it? Maddie thought. Evie never saved anything.

And didn't Maddie have a wish of her own? A big wish?

Maddie had never believed much in wishing. It couldn't hurt to try, though. She held out the penny to make it.

But Evie thought Maddie was giving her the penny. She reached for it, and their fingers touched.

The penny tumbled from their hands. It fell down, down, down and landed in the water with a faint *plop*.

"Evie!" Maddie turned to her sister, annoyed. She couldn't even make a wish without Evie butting in!

"Oops," Evie said.

They both looked down to where the penny had disappeared.

"Oh, well," Maddie said with a sigh. "It was only a penny."

CHAPTER

TWO

"Where have you two been?" Dad asked when Maddie and Evie came into the kitchen a short time later. He was standing by the stove, stirring a pot of spaghetti sauce. "Go ahead and set the table. Dinner is almost ready."

Maddie sniffed the spicy sauce. She suddenly felt very hungry. "We were exploring," she said as she went to the kitchen sink to wash her hands.

"We found a wishing well!" Evie exclaimed.

"You mean that old well down by the barn?" Dad said. "Funny thing, isn't it?"

"What's funny about it?" Maddie asked. She dried her hands, then went to the cupboard. She took out plates and glasses.

"It's very old, much older than the house and the barn," Dad said.

"So?" said Maddie.

"So you don't see wells like that around here," Dad explained. "We don't have any idea who built it."

"Mmm. Smells good," Mom said, coming into the kitchen. "What are you all talking about?"

"We found a wishing well," Evie said.

A little furrow appeared between Mom's eyebrows. "Wells are dangerous, girls. You be careful playing around there."

"We weren't playing, Mama. We were *wishing*," Evie explained.

"Playing or wishing," Mom said. "Just be cautious, please."

"Speaking of wishing, I *wish* Evie would wash her hands and help Maddie set the table," Dad said. "Because dinner is served."

That night at bedtime, Evie came into Maddie's room. "I can't find my book," she said.

Maddie looked up from her own book. She was reading the *Illustrated Encyclopedia of Horses.* "What book?" she asked.

"My fairy-tale book! I can't fall asleep without it," Evie said.

"Where did you last see it?" Maddie asked.

Evie frowned, thinking. "I had it when we went to the barn and . . . oh, the wishing well!"

"There you go. It must still be there." Maddie went back to reading.

But Evie didn't leave. She stood next to Maddie's bed, gazing at her with hopeful eyes.

Maddie looked up again. "What?"

"Will you get it for me?"

"Evie!"

"Please, Maddie," Evie begged. "It's dark outside. It's *spooky*."

Maddie looked out the window. The sun had set. The sky was twilight blue. It was not dark yet, but it would be soon.

It would only take a few minutes to run down to the well. Arguing with Evie would probably take longer.

"Okay. But you owe me one." Maddie swung her feet off her bed. She pulled on her sneakers.

Outside, the wind was blowing. It spun the horse-shaped weather vane on top of the barn. It stirred the grass and trees.

22

Even before she got to the well, Maddie could see the book of fairy tales. It was lying open on the edge.

Maddie paused. From where she stood, it looked like the pages were turning, as if being moved by an invisible hand.

It's just the wind, she told herself. *The wind is turning the pages.*

Maddie hurried to the well. She picked the book up and snapped it shut.

But as she turned to leave, she could have sworn she heard a sound like someone sighing.

She looked around. "Hello?" she murmured. "Is anyone there?"

The only reply was the rustling leaves. The grass whispered and waved.

Maddie shivered. Clutching the book to her chest, she hurried back toward the warm lights of the farmhouse.

Early the next morning, Maddie woke to the sound of a whinny.

That sounds like a horse, she thought sleepily. She rolled over and pulled up the covers.

A second later, she sat up in bed. *That sounds like a horse!*

But *what* horse? The nearest farm was half a mile away. But the sound had come from right outside.

Soft gray light came through the curtains.

Maddie tiptoed over to the window and peeked out.

She rubbed her eyes. Was she dreaming?

A horse was standing below her window.

The horse was white with a blond mane and tail. A brown saddle covered his back. He looked around as if he wondered where he was.

Maddie squealed. It had actually happened! Her parents had gotten a horse!

She threw on her slippers and ran downstairs. Her parents were in the kitchen, drinking coffee.

"Thank you, Dad! Thank you! Thank you!" Maddie gave him a big hug.

Dad looked confused. "You're . . . welcome?"

Maddie hugged her mom. "He's perfect, Mom. I promise I'll take such good care of him."

"Take care of who?" Mom asked.

"What's going on?" Evie appeared in the doorway, yawning.

Maddie was so happy she hugged Evie, too. "We got a horse!"

Dad choked on his coffee. "We did?"

Mom sighed. "Oh, Maddie. Not the horse again. We told you we're just not ready for a—"

A loud whinny cut her off.

Mom raised her eyebrows at Maddie. Everyone jumped up and ran outside.

"What in the world . . . ?" Mom said.

The horse had his nose to the ground. He was sniffing as if he was trying to catch a scent. But when the family came out, he leaped to attention. Maddie got her first good look at him.

He was snowy white all over, except for his muzzle, which was gray. He had a thick, powerful neck and strong legs. When the sunlight touched his golden mane it almost seemed to glow.

Maddie's heart did a cartwheel in her chest. He was the most magnificent horse she'd ever seen.

The horse looked at the Phillipses and frowned.

Maddie had never seen a horse frown before. But this one did. He looked down his regal nose and

snorted. It was a snort that seemed to say, *Pajamas outside? Very undignified!*

After giving them the once-over, the horse seemed to decide Maddie and her family were not important. He went back to sniffing the ground.

"What is this horse doing here?" Dad demanded.

"You mean, you didn't get him?" Maddie asked.

"No." Dad looked at Mom. "Did you?"

"Of course not," Mom said. "I guess he wandered over from another farm. He's wearing a saddle. I wonder if he lost his rider."

"I'm pretty sure he's an Andalusian," Maddie said.

"Nope. He's definitely a horse," Evie said.

"Andalusian is a breed, silly," Maddie said. "A very noble breed. Kings and queens used to keep them."

"I'll call the neighbors and see if anyone is missing a horse," Mom said. "Someone grab him before he wanders off again." The horse was already roaming away.

"I'll do it!" Maddie hurried over to grab the horse's reins.

As she did, she noticed a bronze medallion in the center of his breastplate. It was engraved with

a blazing sun. Maddie leaned closer to read the name on it.

"*Maximus.* Is that your name?" she asked.

Evie gasped.

"What?" Maddie asked, turning to her.

Evie didn't answer. She was running back into the house.

"Come on, Maximus." Maddie led him toward the barn.

In the doorway, Maximus stopped. He looked around the rusty, dusty barn and snorted. There was no mistaking his meaning. *This place is a disgrace.*

"Well, gosh. I know it's not a palace," Maddie said, giving the reins a tug. "But it's not *that* bad."

Evie came running into the barn. She was holding the big book of fairy tales.

"Maddie," she whispered. "It's Rapunzel's horse!"

"Why are you whispering?" Maddie asked.

"Look!" Evie held up the book. It was open to a picture in the story of Rapunzel.

It was the same picture Maddie had been looking at the day before. Three guards on horseback raced through the woods, chasing a thief. The guards wore gleaming bronze uniforms. The horses wore saddles and bridles emblazoned with the symbol of the sun.

Maddie stared. The guards were there. Three brown horses were there.

But the fourth horse—the white one—was gone.

CHAPTER
FOUR

Maddie looked from the horse in the barn to the
picture. She looked from the picture to the horse.

"Oh boy." Maddie rubbed her head. This couldn't
be happening. Horses did not just walk out of
storybooks and into your backyard.

Did they?

No, they did not!

Maddie searched for a logical explanation. She
couldn't think of one.

And wasn't it strange that the horse had turned up right after she'd wished for one?

As if she knew what Maddie was thinking, Evie said, "Do you think it's because of our wish?"

"I was just thinking— Wait." Maddie narrowed her eyes. "What do you mean *our* wish?"

"We both made a wish. On the same penny," Evie explained.

"You wished for a horse?" Maddie was surprised. Since when did Evie care about horses?

"No, I wished for a fairy-tale princess," Evie said matter-of-factly.

"You mean you wished to *be* a princess," Maddie said.

"I wished *for* a princess. To play Princess with me. Because you never want to," Evie explained.

Maddie stared at her. "Evie, that is the nuttiest wish I've ever heard."

"But don't you see?" Evie said. "I wished for a fairy-tale princess. You wished for a horse. And we got—"

They both looked at Maximus. "A fairy-tale horse," the girls said in unison.

Then Maddie shook her head. "It's not possible. I don't believe it. Maximus is just a lost horse.

Mom is probably on the phone talking to his owner right now."

But when Mom came into the barn a few minutes later, she looked puzzled. "I've called all the farms within ten miles. No one is missing a horse."

Evie raised her eyebrows at Maddie as if to say, *You see?*

"Oh boy," Maddie said again.

Mom patted Maximus. "What are we going to do with you?" she asked.

"I can take care of him!" Maddie cried. Here was her chance!

"Oh, Maddie. I don't know. A horse is such a big responsibility. And Dad and I are so busy right now. It's a lot to take on," she said.

"I can do it!" Maddie said. "Please, Mom. Let me try."

Her mom thought it over. Maddie was sure she was going to say no.

But then, to her surprise, Mom nodded. "I guess it would be all right. Just until we find his owner. I'll call the feed-and-tack store in town and see what we need. Welcome to Horsetail Hollow, Maximus."

Mom headed for the barn door. When she got there, she gave Maddie and Maximus one last glance. "Just try not to fall in love with him, sweetie. He'll have to go home, eventually."

Maddie nodded. But she wasn't really listening. Her mind was already spinning with ideas.

However it had happened, her wish had come true. She had a horse to take care of. And what a horse! She couldn't wait to feed him and pet him and put flowers in his beautiful mane.

Maddie beamed at Maximus. This was going to be so great.

CHAPTER
FIVE

Maddie pulled a piece of paper from her back pocket. That morning, she had made a list of everything Maximus needed to be a healthy, happy horse. She read it aloud as she checked it off.

"Good food—check," Maddie said, making a mark with a pencil. "Clean water—check. Comfy stall—check. And, last but not least, a great friend. *Check!*" She drew a smiley face next to the last line.

"What friend?" Evie asked, peeking at the list.

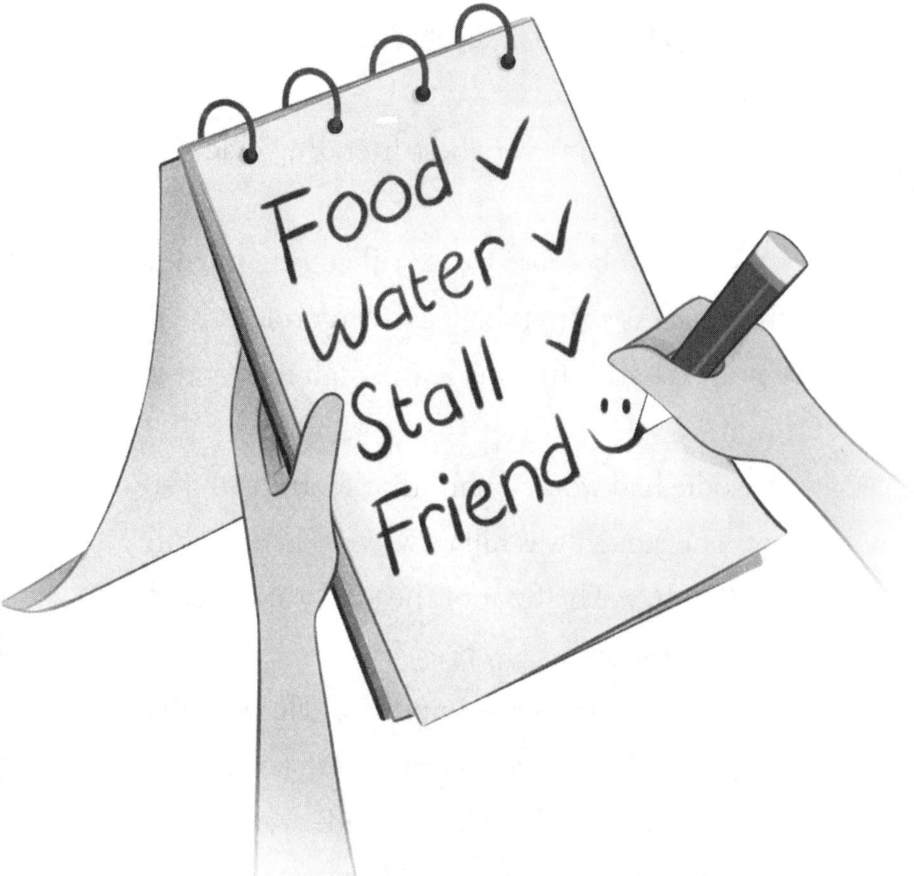
Food
Water
Stall
Friend

"Me, of course!" Maddie said. "Maximus and I are going to be best friends. Aren't we, pal?"

Maximus looked down his nose at her. She could have sworn he raised an eyebrow. *Oh, really?* his face seemed to say.

"He doesn't look very best-friendly," Evie remarked.

"That's just because we're still getting to know each other. As soon as he feels comfortable, he'll warm up. That's why I made this stall nice and cozy for him."

Maddie had worked hard that morning to get it ready. The trough was full of water. The food bin was full of hay. The floor of the stall was covered in fresh, clean straw.

But Maximus was not impressed. He carefully inspected each and every corner. He blew dust off the window ledge. He swiped a spiderweb away with his tail. He chased away a fly. He rearranged the straw so it looked neat and tidy.

Finally, he gave a resigned sigh, as if to say, *I suppose this will have to do.*

"Wow," Maddie said. "I've never seen a horse be so neat."

When he was done with his stall, Maximus turned to them. He looked Maddie and Evie over with a frown.

With his nose, he nudged their chins. *Chins up.*

He flicked his tail against their shoulders. *Shoulders back.*

He poked their bellies. *Don't slouch—stand tall!*

Maximus looked them over again. He gave an approving snort. *Better.*

Maddie looked at Evie. "Did he just fix our . . . posture?" So far, this wasn't going exactly as she'd imagined. There had to be some way to win Maximus over.

"I know what we need," Maddie said. "Treats!"

She ran to the house and got two apples. Back in the barn, she gave one to Evie.

"Watch me," she told Evie. "Here, Maximus. Good horsey. I have an apple for you!"

Maximus's eyes lit up. *Apple?*

Maddie grinned. Yes! It was working! He was coming to her! She held the fruit out on the palm of her hand.

Maximus stopped.

He looked at the apple. He looked at Maddie.

Maddie waved the apple hopefully. "Go on. Take a bite."

Maximus's head drew back. His lip curled. *You want me to eat from your hand? Revolting.* He nodded toward his food trough. *Place the apple there.*

"Oh. Okay." Maddie meekly put it in his trough. Maximus chomped it down in one bite. Then he turned to Evie, eyeing her apple.

"Catch, Maximus!" Evie tossed the apple in the air. Maximus caught it. In seconds, it too was gone.

"That was fun!" Evie said. "I like feeding horses."

Maddie felt a twinge of disappointment. She had always loved feeding horses by hand. She loved the velvety feel of their lips.

But Maximus didn't like that. So what? There were other ways to bond with a horse. Like grooming!

Maddie found a mane brush among the tools in the barn. She couldn't wait to braid Maximus's gorgeous mane. Maybe she'd even put a bow on his tail.

But the moment she put the brush to his mane, Maximus nudged her arm. *STOP!*

"What?" said Maddie.

Maximus shook his mane and whinnied.

"I don't understand," Maddie said.

Maximus rolled his eyes. He blew his forelock off his head. *How could I be more clear?*

"He wants it combed to the left," Evie said.

Maximus nodded. *Exactly.*

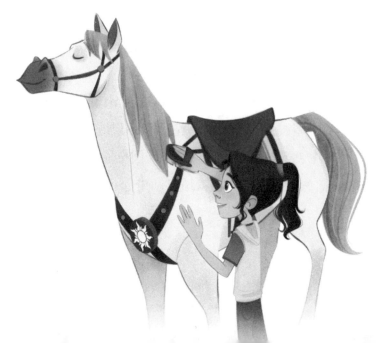

Maddie looked at Evie. "How do you know that?"

Evie shrugged. "It looks better that way."

Maddie brushed the horse's mane to the other side. When all the hair lay smooth along Maximus's neck, she stepped back. "Now you're beautiful—"

Maximus snorted.

"I mean, *handsome*," Maddie said quickly. "Now for the best part! I'll just add a few nice little braids—"

Maximus's head jerked. He whinnied loudly.

"Okay, okay! No braids!" Maddie frowned. Was there anything this horse *wasn't* picky about?

She sighed and set the brush down. This wasn't turning out to be as much fun as she'd thought.

But treats and grooming weren't all there was to having a horse, Maddie reminded herself. The best part was riding! She had a vision of galloping through a field with the wind flying through her hair.

"Come on," Maddie said, leading Maximus out of the barn. "We're going for a ride."

Evie followed them outside. She sat on the paddock fence to watch.

Maddie tried to put her foot in the stirrup. But it was too high off the ground.

Maximus looked back at her. He rolled his eyes. *Seriously?*

"Ergh!" Maddie grunted. "Evie, help me!"

With Evie pushing and Maddie pulling, she made it into the saddle—on her belly.

Maddie couldn't see Maximus's face. But he made his feelings clear. His tail whipped around and spanked her.

Evie giggled.

"Ha-ha. Very funny." Maddie wriggled around until she was sitting upright. She took hold of the reins. "Okay, Maximus. Let's go!"

Maximus didn't budge.

"I said, giddyup!" Maddie nudged him with her heels.

Maximus just stood there.

Maddie nudged harder. She ordered, then she pleaded. She cried and cajoled. But Maximus could not be moved. He just stood there with his head held high, lashing her with his tail.

At last, worn out from trying, Maddie slid down from his back.

The regal horse looked down at her. His expression seemed to say, *I am a horse of the Royal Guard. I do not take commands. I give them.*

With a swish of his tail, Maximus strolled back to the barn.

Maddie watched him go. She was starting to get the feeling that Maximus was *not* the horse she had dreamed of.

But he was a horse. And a horse could be trained.

With a little work, Maddie would make him the horse of her dreams.

CHAPTER
SIX

For the next few days, Maddie tried her best with
Maximus.

Each morning, she woke early to bring the
horse his bucket of oats. Maximus kept a very strict
schedule. He was up at daybreak. And if Maddie was
ever late with breakfast, he stamped his hoof and
scolded her with a gruff snort.

While Maddie tidied his stall, Maximus went for

a trot around the paddock. He always did exactly ten laps.

After his exercise, Maddie brushed and groomed Maximus. She picked his hooves, which made him whinny. (He had ticklish feet.) She brought him carrots and apples.

But no matter how hard she tried to make him feel at home, Maximus never seemed to relax. He didn't frolic or nibble grass like other horses. He just marched back and forth along the fence, swishing his tail. He watched over the farm like a guard watching a castle.

If Maximus saw crows on the fence, he chased them off. If he saw squirrels stealing nuts, he stamped his hooves to scare them away. He kept a distrustful eye on Ramsey. Maximus had taken an instant disliking to the goat. The two had long staring contests that always ended with Ramsey head-butting the fence.

And Maximus was so bossy! Every time he saw Maddie, he nudged her with his nose. *Chin up. Shoulders back. Don't slouch—stand tall!*

Maddie was starting to think she wasn't training Maximus. *He* was training *her.*

"How are things going with Maximus?" Maddie's dad asked one day when Maddie came back from cleaning Maximus's stall.

Maddie's parents were sitting on the farmhouse porch with Evie. They were taking a break from painting the house.

Maddie plopped down next to them. She sighed heavily. "Okay, I guess."

"Just okay?" Mom asked.

"It's not really how I thought having a horse would be," Maddie admitted. "Maximus is a lot of work."

"I've always said a horse is a big responsibility," Mom said.

"It's not that. Maximus is so stubborn. He has all these opinions. He thinks everything has to be a certain way," Maddie explained.

Her parents glanced at each other and smiled. "That sounds like someone I know," Dad said.

Maddie shook her head. They weren't getting it. "Have you ever heard of a horse who wants his mane brushed only to the left?" she asked. "Sometimes he doesn't even seem like a horse."

"I like having Maximus around," Dad said. "He's been very helpful with the house painting. He pointed out all the spots I missed."

"He does keep an eye on things," Mom agreed.

"And he's good at hide-and-seek," Evie added. "He always finds me!"

"What I think is strange is that no one has come to get him," Mom said. "I've put up ads all over the community. I even spoke to the local vet. No one seems to know where he came from."

Maddie and Evie glanced uneasily at each other. "Er, yeah. It's a real mystery," Maddie said.

"I'll help you with Maximus, Maddie," Evie offered. "I like grooming!"

"See, there you go." Dad patted Maddie's shoulder. "Don't worry, Maddie. It'll all work out."

The next morning, when Maddie came out to the
barnyard, she saw Evie sitting on the fence rail.
Evie was wearing a ruffled yellow gown and her
princess crown. She talked to Maximus while she
groomed him.

"I would say Rapunzel is in my top three
princesses." Evie picked up a handful of mane and
stuffed it into a ponytail. "She has the best hair. I
wonder how Rapunzel washes her hair. Do you think

she hangs it out the window when it rains? What if it stops raining before she gets the shampoo out?" Evie braided a strand of Maximus's mane. She tied a bow onto the end of it.

She picked up a hand mirror and held it out for the horse to see. "All done, Maximus. Do you like it?"

Maximus looked at his reflection. His mouth fell open. *Are you kidding me?*

He shook his mane until all the braids and ponytails flew out.

"That was naughty," Evie scolded, wagging a finger. "Now we have to start over."

Maddie snatched the brush away. "What are you doing?"

"I'm helping," Evie said.

"Some help!" Maddie looked at Maximus's messy mane. "It's worse than before you started."

"We'll have to finish later," Evie said. "Right now it's time for my fencing lesson."

"Your *what?*" exclaimed Maddie.

"Maximus is teaching me," Evie said. She picked up two sticks and handed one to Maximus. He took it between his teeth.

Evie raised her stick. "On guard!" she shouted.

Maximus raised his stick, too.

"Too-shay!" Evie thrust her stick at Maximus. He met it with his own.

Clack. Clack. Clack. Their sticks rattled together. They slashed and parried like two swordfighters.

"Arr!" Evie shouted. "Don't mess with this princess!"

Maddie could not believe what she was seeing. This was NOT horselike behavior!

"STOP!" she yelled.

Maximus and Evie froze. They looked at her in surprise.

"Horses are supposed to frolic! They are supposed to nibble carrots. They are supposed to be your best friend!" Maddie pointed at Maximus. "You do none of those things! You are a BAD HORSE!"

Maximus's mouth fell open. The stick dropped to the ground. *No one has ever called me that before!*

Maddie turned and ran. When she got to her bedroom, she threw herself down on the bed.

I give up! she thought. *Maximus will never be the horse of my dreams. A royal horse? Ha! A royal pain is more like it.*

All Maddie wanted was a horse she could play with and ride. Was that too much to ask? Ooh, she wished she could un-wish that wish!

Maddie sat up. Why hadn't she thought of that before?

The wishing well had worked once, hadn't it? Why wouldn't it work again? She could send Maximus back to wherever he'd come from. She could wish for the horse of her dreams.

All for only a penny!

Maddie got her money jar down from the shelf. She unscrewed the lid and took out a penny.

Maddie looked at the coin in her hand. She thought about Maximus. Was she giving up on him too soon?

Where there's a will, there's a way, Maddie thought. It was something her parents always said.

"Where there's a *well*, there's a way, too," she said. She put the penny in her pocket.

As she left the house, Maddie let the door slam. Evie and Maximus looked up from their fencing match. But Maddie didn't even glance their way.

She walked across the barnyard, headed for the woods and the well.

She passed Ramsey's pen. "BLAH!" the goat bleated.

"Blah yourself, you stinky old—"

Maddie stopped. The pen was open. And Ramsey was not in it.

Maddie slowly turned around. Ramsey was on the other side of the barnyard, watching her with his yellow eyes. Maddie could have sworn he smiled.

Ramsey lowered his horns and charged.

She looked left and right, but there was nowhere to run. In a panic, Maddie squeezed her eyes shut. She could hear hooves pounding the ground. *Please don't hit me. Please don't hit me*, she prayed. The pounding hooves got closer. They were right next to her. But . . .

She opened her eyes. Maximus was standing between Ramsey and Maddie. He was protecting

her! With a fearsome whinny, he reared onto his hind legs.

Ramsey tried to head-butt Maximus. But the horse was too quick. He dodged sideways, then circled around, driving Ramsey back into his pen.

Maximus slammed the gate. Maddie flipped the latch. *And stay there!* the horse whinnied.

Ramsey head-butted the gate. But he was trapped.

Maximus turned to Maddie. He nosed her, as if to say, *Are you okay?*

"You saved my life!" Maddie said in amazement.

He lowered his head modestly. *All in the line of duty.*

"You *do* care." Maddie petted him. She kissed his nose. She scratched him under the chin. "You are a good horse, Maximus. More than good. You are the *best* horse ever."

Maximus sighed happily. He swished his tail, as if to say that all he'd ever wanted was to be appreciated.

CHAPTER

EIGHT

"Good morning, Maximus!" Maddie said as she came into the barn to give him his oats.

Maximus hung his head out of his stall and whinnied. *Good morning!*

"Look what I brought you." Maddie held up a shiny red apple.

Maximus's eyes lit up. *Apple!*

Maddie carefully placed it in his trough. "Enjoy, buddy."

She smiled as she watched him eat. She no longer cared about getting Maximus to eat from her hand. When Maddie gave it some thought, she realized she wouldn't want to eat from someone's hand either.

Something had changed since the day Ramsey escaped from his pen. Maddie had stopped seeing only the things she didn't like about Maximus, and started seeing the things she *did* like. Maximus was stern and fussy, but he was also loyal, kindhearted, and brave. What more could you want in a friend?

After Maximus had finished breakfast, Maddie said, "I have a surprise for you."

She brought in his saddle. Maddie had stayed up late polishing it until Maximus could see his reflection in the shine.

When Maximus saw it, he whinnied with joy.

Maddie helped him put it on. She fastened the girth tight.

Maximus looked down at her. He tossed his head, as if to say, *Want a ride?*

"Really?" Maddie asked. She hadn't been in the saddle since the first day he'd arrived.

Maximus nodded.

Maddie put her foot in the stirrup. It took her three tries, but she finally got up. This time, Maximus waited patiently.

He glanced back at her. *Ready?*

"Ready!" Maddie took the reins.

Maximus raised his head. *Chin up!*

He flicked her with his tail. *Shoulders back!*

He straightened his neck. *Don't slouch—sit tall.*

"Oh!" Maddie gasped, suddenly understanding. "Maximus, you've been trying to teach me how to ride this whole time!"

Maximus nickered. *Of course. I am a horse of high standards, after all.*

And they were off. First they walked. Then they trotted. The next thing Maddie knew, they were galloping across the field with the wind in their hair.

They rode together the rest of the day. And when he was sure no one was looking, Maximus even let her put a flower in his mane.

One day, when Maddie and Maximus returned from their morning ride, Evie was waiting for them. She had the book of fairy tales, and she looked upset.

"Maddie!" Evie cried. "Something happened to Rapunzel!"

"What do you mean?" Maddie asked as she climbed down from the saddle.

Evie opened to the story of Rapunzel. "Look at the pictures," she said.

The story started as it always had, with Baby Rapunzel, the princess born with magical golden hair. Maddie turned the page. Here was the picture of the witch kidnapping Rapunzel, and the tower where she hid the young princess.

Maddie came to the page that showed guardsmen on horses racing through the forest. She traced her finger over the place where Maximus had once been.

Maximus looked over her shoulder. He whinnied in surprise. *Hey, I know that place!*

On the next page, Rapunzel was a young woman. She leaned out of the window of her tower prison,

gazing at the world with bright green eyes. Her long blond hair floated down from the tower. It looked like a banner waving in the breeze. But the picture looked faded, as if it had been left out in the sun.

On the next page, the image was even fainter. And the next page was so faint, Maddie could hardly see it at all.

The last several pages were blank. It was as if that part of the story had been erased.

"What did you do to the book?" Maddie asked Evie.

"I didn't do anything! What if it was our wish, Maddie?" Evie whispered. "We took Maximus out of the story. What if without him, the story can't have its happy ending? What if Rapunzel is still trapped in the tower—and it's our fault?"

"No." Maddie shook her head. She didn't want to believe it. "You just left it outside for too long. That's why the pictures are fading. It doesn't have anything to do with us."

"Maddie." Evie looked at her with big, worried eyes. "Rapunzel needs Maximus. She needs him to get to her happily-ever-after."

What about my *happily-ever-after?* Maddie wanted to say. She had waited so long for a horse of her own. She finally had one, and he was perfect. Did she really have to give him up?

She looked back at the picture of the horses in the forest.

Maddie blinked. Then she squinted.

In the background, so small she'd almost missed it, was the wishing well. *Their* wishing well. The very same one.

"We need to send him home," Maddie said sadly. "Don't we?"

Evie nodded. "But how?"

Maddie thought. "There's a wishing well here." She pointed at the picture. "There's a wishing well *there*. Maybe the same magic that brought Max here can take him home. Maybe we can ask the wishing well."

Evie smiled. "See, Maddie? I knew you believed in magic."

Maximus had been listening to their whole conversation. Suddenly, he snorted, as if he'd come to a decision. Then he turned and trotted away.

He hopped the fence and set out briskly toward the woods. Maddie and Evie ran after him. They caught up with him at the wishing well.

Maddie set the book down on the side of the well. She opened it to the picture of the forest, where Maximus had once been. She didn't know if it mattered. But it seemed like the right thing to do.

"Wait," Maddie said. "I don't have a coin. How can we make a wish?"

Evie reached into her pocket. She held up a penny. "I've been saving one, just in case."

Maddie put her hand on Evie's. Maximus put his hoof on Maddie's hand.

Maddie took a deep breath. "We wish to send Maximus home," she whispered. Together, they tossed the penny.

At first, nothing happened. Then they felt a breeze on their faces. It was coming from the wishing well!

The breeze blew stronger and stronger, until it became a wind. It whipped their hair and spun the horse-shaped weather vane on the barn.

The world around them seemed to spin. Maddie felt dizzy. She squeezed Evie's hand and shut her eyes tight.

As suddenly as it had started, the wind died down.

When Maddie opened her eyes again, Horsetail Hollow was gone.

They were standing in a dense forest. Trees rose high above their heads. The ground beneath their feet was spongy with moss. It wasn't like the woods around Horsetail Hollow. It seemed ancient and wild.

The wishing well was still next to them. It looked as if it had stood in that place for hundreds of years.

This is a dream, Maddie told herself. *I must have slipped and fallen and hit my head. Because if it isn't a dream, that means . . .*

"*We're* in the fairy tale," Evie exclaimed. "Maximus brought us with him!"

CHAPTER

NINE

Ever since they'd made their first wish, a tiny kernel of doubt had remained in Maddie's mind. *Maximus didn't* really *come from a fairy tale,* the doubt said. *It's just a coincidence.* Certainly, Maximus's arrival was unusual. Extraordinary, even. But that didn't *prove* it was magic—or that their wish had really come true.

But as soon as Evie said "We're in the fairy tale!" Maddie's last bit of doubt blew away like dandelion fluff. Because Maddie could see with her own eyes—and hear with her ears, and even smell with her nose—that it was true. The picture from the storybook had come alive around them. She could hear birds trilling. She could feel the squish of the moss under her feet. Even the air smelled different.

They were actually IN a FAIRY TALE!

Evie gasped as something occurred to her. "*Rapunzel* is here! Maddie, we could meet her!" She looked around as if Rapunzel might pop out from behind a tree.

But Maddie was looking at Maximus. A change had come over the horse. He had always been strong and proud. But now he looked positively regal. *I am Maximus,* his face seemed to say, *Captain of the Royal Guard: Horse Division. And I am on the trail of JUSTICE.*

Maximus sniffed the air. His eyes narrowed as if he'd caught a whiff of wrongdoing on the breeze.

Suddenly, he turned and strode off through the trees.

"Maximus?" Maddie hurried after him.

Maximus stopped in front of a large tree. A poster had been nailed to it.

Maddie pulled the poster from the tree. "Do you know this guy?"

Maximus grabbed the poster with his teeth. He began to chew it to bits.

"I'll take that as a yes." Maddie took back the

poster—what was left of it. She turned to her sister. "Hey, Evie! Look at—"

Maddie stopped. Evie wasn't there.

"Evie?" She looked around. "Evie, where are you?"

Maddie's heart began to pound. She'd only been there five minutes, and she'd already lost her little sister! "Maximus, help me find Evie!"

Together they retraced their steps. They searched behind bushes and trees. Evie was nowhere to be found.

Just when Maddie was starting to panic, she heard her name.

"Maddie!" Evie's head poked out from behind some vines. "I found her!"

"Evie!" Maddie cried. "You scared me to death."

"Come quick," Evie said. "This way!"

Maddie and Maximus followed Evie into a tunnel hidden behind the vines. A moment later, they stepped out into sunlight. Maddie gasped.

They were standing in a beautiful hidden canyon. A waterfall spilled down the side of the cliffs into a quiet river below.

A stone tower, tall as a ten-story building, stood in the center of the canyon. At the very top, a young woman sat in a window. Her long golden hair floated out from the tower, rippling in the breeze.

Evie looked starstruck. "Maddie, it's really her— Princess Rapunzel!" she exclaimed.

Her cry echoed off the cliff walls.

Rapunzel peered down from the tower. "Who's there?" she called.

Quickly, Maddie pushed Evie behind a boulder and ducked after her. She waved for Maximus to hide behind a tree.

"Why did you do that?" Evie complained. "I want to meet her."

"Evie, use your head. There's a witch up there," Maddie said. "And I don't think she'll be too happy to see us."

They peeked around the boulder to watch. Sure enough, a moment later, a dark-haired woman appeared in the window next to Rapunzel. "Who are you talking to, flower?" she asked. She had a sharp voice that carried all the way to Maddie and Evie's hiding spot.

"That's Mother Gothel. She's mean!" Evie hissed.

Rapunzel said something they couldn't hear. The witch peered out from the tower. But she didn't spot them in their hiding places.

They watched as Rapunzel used her hair to lower the witch to the ground. The witch headed for the tunnel that Maddie, Evie, and Maximus had just come through. She passed very close to where they were hiding. But she didn't look in their direction.

Maddie sighed in relief. "Whew! That was close. Now what should we— Evie?"

Evie was no longer next to her. Maddie saw her running toward the tower, waving like she'd spotted her best friend.

"Rapunzel! It's me, Evie!" she called.

When Rapunzel saw Evie, she gave a little scream. She yanked her hair back up, and slammed the shutters.

Evie stopped short. "Rapunzel?"

Maddie and Maximus came out from their hiding spots. They all looked up at the closed window.

The shutters opened a crack. "I'm warning you!" Rapunzel called. "I have a frying pan, and I'm not afraid to use it!"

Maddie, Evie, and Maximus looked at one another. "Did she say a *frying pan?*" Maddie asked.

"Who are you and what do you want?" Rapunzel called.

Maddie thought quickly. What should they say? A wishing well brought them from another world? That seemed like a lot to explain.

Better keep it simple, she decided.

"We're travelers from a faraway land," she called.

Rapunzel opened the shutter a bit wider. She

cupped a hand to her ear. "Did you say you're with a traveling band?"

Maddie tried again. "We come from far away!"

Rapunzel peered down at them. She shook her head. "Sorry, I can't come out to play!"

Ugh! They were getting nowhere. Maddie decided to cut to the chase.

"We brought the horse to rescue you!" she yelled.

"I know!" Rapunzel yelled back. "Shouting makes me hoarse, too!"

Maximus reared up on his hind legs. He whinnied loudly.

Rapunzel smiled. "I love your horse!" she called.

"This is ridiculous," Maddie said. "How is Maximus supposed to rescue Rapunzel from the tower when she's up there, and he's down here?"

"Maximus doesn't rescue Rapunzel," Evie said.

Maddie looked at her. "He doesn't?"

Maximus's ears went down. *I don't?*

Evie put her hands on her hips. "If you bothered to read the whole story, Maddie, you'd know. Flynn Rider rescues her from the tower."

When Maximus heard the name Flynn Rider, he bared his teeth. He pawed at the ground. *Let me at that criminal!*

"Flynn Rider? You mean, this Flynn Rider?" Maddie pulled the poster from her pocket. She waved it at Evie.

"That's him!" Evie tilted her head, thoughtfully. "That's not a very good picture, though. His nose looks too big."

"Then what are we even doing here?" Maddie asked. "Evie, you said Rapunzel *needed* Maximus!"

Evie heaved a big sigh. "The palace guards are after Flynn, because Flynn has stolen a royal crown," she explained patiently. "Maximus chases him through the woods, and *that's* how Flynn finds Rapunzel's tower."

"Why didn't you say so?" Maddie cried. "If we want to save this story, we've got to find that thief before someone else does!"

Maddie helped Evie onto Maximus's back. Then she swung into the saddle behind her.

Evie gasped. "I forgot to warn Rapunzel!" As they galloped away, she looked back and shouted, "Rapunzel, Mother Gothel kidnapped you!"

From her tower window, Rapunzel waved. "Good-bye!" she called. "Awful nice meeting you, too!"

CHAPTER
TEN

Maximus charged through the forest. His hooves tore up clods of dirt. His breath steamed.

Maddie leaned forward in the saddle. Evie clung tightly to her waist.

"Go, Maximus! Go!" Maddie cried.

Up! They soared over a log.

Watch out! They ducked under a branch.

Maddie's heart seemed to gallop in her chest.

This wasn't like riding through the meadow with flowers in their hair.

It was better. They were on the trail of JUSTICE! And they were going to save the day.

Maximus slowed. He paused to sniff the ground with his keen nose. When he picked up a scent, he tore off in another direction.

"I think I see him!" Evie exclaimed.

Through a break in the trees ahead, they could see a man coming toward them. He wore old-fashioned clothes and tall boots. A leather satchel

hung across his chest. He was looking back over his shoulder.

Maximus's ears went back. His nostrils flared. He let out a furious whinny. *I'm coming for you, Flynn Rider!*

Flynn Rider looked up. His face darkened. "YOU!" he shouted at Maximus. "BAD HORSE!"

"He is NOT a bad horse!" Maddie exclaimed. "He is the BEST horse!"

Maximus skidded to a stop. They had come to the edge of a narrow ravine. Maddie, Maximus, and Evie were on one side of it. Flynn Rider was on the other.

When Flynn noticed Maddie and Evie, he blinked in surprise. "The palace guards seem to get younger every year."

"We know who you are, Flynn Rider," Maddie cried. "We know what you stole. Now you will meet your destiny."

"So give us that crown!" Evie roared.

"Wait, why do we need the crown? Is that part of the story?" Maddie whispered.

"No," Evie whispered back. "I just want to try it on."

Flynn smiled smugly. "You seem to have missed one important detail," he said. "I'm here. And you're over there."

Maximus took a few steps back. Then he charged toward the ravine.

"What are you doing?" Maddie asked. "Maximus? MAAAAXIMUS!"

With a mighty leap, the horse sailed across the chasm. He landed next to Flynn.

"I wasn't expecting that," the thief admitted.

At that moment, the ground trembled. Two palace guards on horseback burst from the forest behind Flynn. They wore gleaming armor and carried swords.

"There he is!" one of the guards shouted. "Retrieve that crown at any cost!"

Maddie held out a hand to Flynn Rider. "Quick! Get on!" she said.

"What?" The thief looked confused. But with the palace guards bearing down on him, he didn't ask questions. He grabbed Maddie's hand and squeezed onto Maximus behind Evie.

"Go, Maximus!" Maddie cried.

But the horse stamped his foot. *I will not help this thief!*

The guards were closing the distance. They only had a moment.

Maddie leaned forward. "Maximus, listen. You are not just a good horse. You are a HERO."

Both of Maximus's ears swiveled toward her. *HERO?*

"You have a *destiny*," Maddie told him. "You will help save the princess and bring joy to the kingdom. But it starts with saving this thief."

Maximus gave a resigned sigh. *I'll do it. But I won't like it.*

He took a few steps back.

Just as the palace guards reached them, Maximus made another death-defying leap. He soared over the ravine, carrying all three of them.

"Bye-bye!" Evie waved back at the guards as Maximus galloped away.

When they were close to the cave that hid Rapunzel's tower, they stopped and let Flynn off.

"Thank you, kids, for saving my hide back there—" Flynn started to say.

Maddie cut him off. "Don't thank us. You better run, thief!"

"Wait, what?" Flynn gaped at her in confusion. "I thought you were helping me."

Maddie held tight to the reins. Maximus was chomping at the bit as if he wanted to chomp Flynn. She wasn't sure he was pretending. "You'd better find a place to hide. A really good place."

"Yeah!" Evie said toughly. "Like maybe in a *tunnel* hidden behind *vines*."

"If you hurry, I *might* not sic my horse on you," Maddie added. She leaned forward and whispered to Flynn, "Trust me. It's for your own good."

Flynn stared at her. He gave his head a little shake, then hurried away.

They watched him go. "For Pete's sake," Maddie said. "He's not even going in the right direction. Do we have to do everything?"

"I told him, *tunnel* behind *vines*! Grown-ups never listen," Evie complained.

"Come on, Maximus," Maddie said, urging him forward. "We'd better round him up."

Maximus whinnied. *With pleasure.*

When the thief saw the big white horse coming after him, he started to run. Maximus herded him toward the hidden tunnel, just like he'd herded Ramsey back into his pen. They zigzagged through the woods, until Flynn was aimed at the secret entrance.

Finally, Flynn dove inside.

"Yeesh!" Maddie said. "It took him long enough. Are we sure he's going to find Rapunzel?"

"We'd better watch," Evie said.

Maddie and Evie climbed down from Maximus's back. The three of them hurried through the tunnel.

When they reached the canyon, they saw Flynn scaling the tower wall. Up, up, up he climbed. At last, he disappeared through the window.

From inside, there came a loud *BONK!*

Maddie winced. "I think Rapunzel *did* say 'a frying pan.' Evie, are you sure this is how the story goes?"

"Yep," said Evie. "Now all they have to do is get down from the tower, escape the palace guards, fall in love, defeat Mother Gothel, and return to the castle so the whole kingdom can celebrate!"

Maddie glanced doubtfully at the tower window. "They don't seem to be off to a very good start."

Maximus snorted in agreement.

"We did what we had to do. We got Flynn to Rapunzel," Maddie said. "It's time for us to go home. Mom and Dad must be really worried."

Together they walked back through the tunnel. The wishing well was just ahead, waiting for them. Maddie and Evie walked toward it.

But when Maddie looked back, Maximus was still standing near the entrance to the tunnel.

"Max?" Maddie said.

Maximus lowered his head. He looked at her sadly.

"You're not coming with us, are you?" Maddie murmured. She didn't need an answer. She already knew.

Maximus didn't belong on a farm. His place was here. This story needed a hero. And Max needed to fulfill his destiny.

Maddie went to Maximus. She scratched him under the chin and kissed his soft nose.

"You are the best horse I've ever known. I will never forget how you saved me from Ramsey.

I'm . . ." Maddie felt a lump in her throat. She swallowed hard. "I'm really going to miss you."

Maximus nuzzled her cheek.

"Don't forget us," Maddie whispered.

Maximus nickered. *Never.*

Evie hugged Maximus. "Take care of Rapunzel, okay? Make sure she and Flynn get to their happily-ever-after."

Maximus nuzzled Evie, too. Then he gently nudged them in the direction of the wishing well.

Evie took another penny from her pocket. She held Maddie's hand as they made the wish that would take them home.

As the wind started to blow, they looked back at Maximus.

The horse lifted his nose. He swished his tail.

Chin up.

Shoulders back.

Stand tall!

And then—*whoosh!* They were gone.

Maddie and Evie found themselves back in Horsetail Hollow, standing beside the wishing well. The day was calm and bright. A light breeze blew across the farm, carrying the smell of fresh-cut grass.

The fairy-tale book lay open on the edge of the well, right where they'd left it. Maddie picked it up.

Maximus was back in his place in the picture. As he charged through the forest, the horse's nostrils flared and his lips curled back in a fierce grimace.

But she could tell from the shine in his eyes that he was happy. He was where he belonged, on the trail of justice and good.

"What about Rapunzel?" Evie asked.

Maddie turned the pages. Before their eyes, Rapunzel's story began to return. Letter by letter, words appeared, marching along like lines of tiny ants. Colorful pictures bloomed across the page like flowers opening. They saw Rapunzel and Flynn meet, escape from the tower, and finally fall in love.

"We did it," said Evie. "We fixed the story!"

"Maximus did it," Maddie said. "He's the real hero. We just went along for the ride." She looked at the picture of Rapunzel and Flynn. "I'm sorry you never got to play Princess with Rapunzel, Evie."

Evie shrugged. "It's okay. I had more fun with you and Maximus. I'm really going to miss him."

"Me too," Maddie said sadly.

She closed the book and tucked it under her arm.

"I know what will cheer us up. How about I read you a story?"

Evie's face lit up. "Really? All the words?"

"All of them," Maddie promised. "I want to see how this story ends."

Maddie and Evie lay in a big pile of hay. The big book of fairy tales lay open between them. A ray of sunlight spilled through the open hayloft door, warming their faces, as Maddie read the ending of Rapunzel's story.

"'Rapunzel and her true love returned to the castle, where the king and queen welcomed them with open arms. The kingdom was so glad to have their princess back that the celebration lasted a week. And Rapunzel, when she became queen, was

as good and fair and kind a ruler as anyone could hope for.'"

"And . . ." Evie chimed in.

"'They all lived happily ever after,'" the sisters read in unison.

Evie sighed with satisfaction.

Maddie traced her finger over the picture of Maximus. He was standing next to Rapunzel and Flynn on their wedding day. They had made him Horse of Honor.

"I'm really going to miss him," she said. "But it's funny, he doesn't seem that far away. I can almost hear him nickering."

"I can almost smell his nice, horsey smell," Evie agreed.

"I feel like any moment, I could hear him call," Maddie said.

From below in the barn, there came a loud whinny.

The girls looked at each other. Then they
scrambled to the edge of the hayloft and
looked down.

A huge horse stood below them in the barn. He
had a coal-black body, a thick mane, and great tufts
of white fur above his hooves. He opened his mouth
and gave a fretful whinny, as if to say, *Where am I?*

Maddie's mouth fell open. "I can't believe it."

Evie grinned. "Our wish came true—again!"